John Cunliffe's
GIANT
STORIES

John Cunliffe's
Giant
stories

Illustrated by
Fritz Wegner

Scholastic Children's Books,
Scholastic Publications Ltd,
7-9 Pratt Street, London NW1 0AE

Scholastic Inc.,
555 Broadway, New York, NY 10012-3999, USA

Scholastic Canada Ltd,
123 Newkirk Road, Richmond Hill,
Ontario, Canada L4C 4G5

Ashton Scholastic Pty Ltd,
PO Box 579, Gosford, New South Wales,
Australia

Ashton Scholastic Ltd,
Private Bag 92801, Penrose, Auckland,
New Zealand

First published by André Deutsch as GIANT KIPPERNOSE AND
OTHER STORIES, 1972
First published in this edition by Scholastic Publications Ltd, 1994

Copyright © John Cunliffe 1972 and 1994

ISBN 0 590 55719 X

Printed by Cox & Wyman Ltd, Reading, Berks.

All rights reserved

10 9 8 7 6 5 4 3 2 1

Contents

One

The story of Giant Kippernose

Once there was a giant called Kippernose. He lived on a lonely farm in the mountains. He was not fierce. Indeed he was as kind and gentle as a giant could be. He liked children, and was fond of animals. He was good at telling stories. His favourite foods were ice-cream, cakes, lollipops and sausages. He would help anyone, large or small. And yet he had no friends. When he went to the town to do his shopping, everyone ran away from him. Busy streets emptied in a trice. Everyone ran home, bolted their doors and closed all their windows, even on hot summer days.

Kippernose shouted, 'Don't run away! I'll not hurt you! Please don't run away, I like little people. I've only come to do my shopping. Please come out. I'll tell you a good story about a dragon and a mermaid.'

But it was no use. The town stayed silent and empty; the doors and windows stayed firmly shut. Poor Kippernose wanted so much to have someone to talk to. He felt so lonely that he often sat down in the town square and cried his heart out. You would think someone would take pity on him, but no one ever did. He simply could not understand it. He even tried going to another town, far across the mountains, but just the same thing happened.

'Has all the world gone mad?' said Kippernose to himself, and took his solitary way home.

The truth was that the people were not afraid of Kippernose, and they had not gone mad, either. The truth was. . . that Kippernose had not had a single bath in a hundred years, or more! The poor fellow carried such a stink wherever he went that everyone with a nose on his face ran for cover at the first whiff. Oh, how that giant reeked! Pooh, you could smell him a mile away, and worst of all on hot days. People buried their noses in flowers and lavender-bags, but still the stench crept in. The wives cried shame and shame upon him, and swore that his stink turned their milk sour, and their butter rancid. What made matters worse, he never washed his hair or his whiskers, either. Smelly whiskers bristled all over his chin and little creatures crept through them. His greasy hair fell down his back. He never used a comb. He never brushed his teeth. *And*, quite often, he went to bed with his boots on.

When he was a boy, Kippernose was always

clean and smart, his mother saw to that. Long long ago, his good mother had gone off to live in far Cathay, and he had forgotten all she had told him about keeping clean and tidy, and changing his socks once a week. It was a lucky thing when his socks wore out, because that was the only time he would change them. He had no notion of the sight and smell he was. He never looked in a mirror. His smell had grown up with him, and he didn't notice it at all. His mind was deep among tales of dragons and wizards, for people in stories were his only friends. If only someone could have told him about his smell, in a nice way, all would have been well. The people grumbled enough amongst themselves.

Mrs Dobson, of Ivy Cottage, was one of them. Friday was market day, and ironing day too, and every Friday night she would bang her iron angrily, and say to quiet Mr Dobson by the fireside, 'That giant's a scandal. It's every market day we have the sickening stench of him, and the whole pantry turned sour and rotten, too. Can't you men do something about it? You sit there and warm your toes, and nod off to sleep, while the world's going to ruin. . .'

'But, Bessie, my dear,' mild Mr Dobson answered, 'what can we do? You cannot expect anyone to go up to an enormous giant and say – I say, old chap, you smell most dreadfully – now can you? Besides, no one could get near enough to him – the smell would drive them away.'

'You could send him a letter,' said Mrs Dobson.

'But he can't read. He never went to school. Even as a boy, Kippernose was too big to get through the school door, my old grandfather used to say.'

'Well, the government should do something about it,' said Mrs Dobson, banging on. 'If that Queen of ours came out of her palace and took a sniff of our Kippernose, *she'd* do something quickly enough, I'll bet.'

But it was not the Queen, or the government, or Mr Dobson, who solved the problem in the end. It was a creature so small that no one could see it.

One Friday in the middle of winter, a cold day of ice and fog, Kippernose went to town to do his shopping as usual. He felt so unhappy that he didn't even bother to call out and ask the people to stay to talk to him. He just walked gloomily into the market-place.

'It's no good,' he said to himself, 'they'll never be friends with me. They don't seem to think a giant has feelings like anyone else. I might just as well be. . .'

'Hoi! Look where you're going!' an angry voice shouted up from the foggy street. 'Oh, I say, oh, help!' Then there was a great crash, and there were apples rolling everywhere. Then a babble of voices gathered round Kippernose.

'The clumsy great oaf – look he's knocked Jim Surtees' apple-cart over. Did you ever see such a mess? Tramping about, not looking where he's going, with his head in the sky.'

Amidst all this angry noise stood Kippernose, with an enormous smile spreading across his big face. The smile grew to a grin.

'*They're not running away.* They're *not running away,*' said Kippernose, in a joyous whisper. Then he bent down, right down, and got down on his knees to bring his face near to the people.

'Why aren't you running away from me?' he said, softly, so as not to frighten them. 'Why aren't you running away as you always do? Please tell me, I beg of you.'

Jim Surtees was so angry that he had no fear of Kippernose, and he climbed on to his overturned apple-cart, and shouted up at him, 'Why, you great fool, it's because we cannot *smell* you.'

'Smell?' said Kippernose, puzzled.

'Yes. Smell, stink, pong, stench, call it what you like,' said Jim.

'But I don't smell,' said Kippernose.

'Oh, yes you do!' all the people shouted together.

'You stink,' shouted Jim. 'You stink to the very

heavens. That's why everyone runs away from you. It's too much for us – we just *have* to run away.'

'Why can't you smell me today?' said Kippernose.

'Because we've all caught a cold in the head for the first time in our lives, and our noses are stuffed up and runny, and we cannot smell anything, that's why,' said Jim. 'Some merchant came from England, selling ribbons, and gave us his germs as well. So we can't smell you today, but next week we'll be better, and then see how we'll run.'

'But what can I do?' said Kippernose, looking so sad that even Jim felt sorry for him. 'I'm so lonely with no one to talk to.'

'Well, you could take a bath,' said Jim.

'And you could wash your whiskers,' said Mrs Dobson. '. . . and your hair,' she added.

'*And* you could wash your clothes,' said Mr Dobson.

'*And* change your socks,' said Mrs Fox, eyeing his feet.

Distant memories stirred in Kippernose's head. 'Yes. Oh . . . yes. Mother did say something about all that, once, long ago, but I didn't take much notice. Do I really smell as badly as all that? Do I really?'

'Oh yes, you certainly do,' said Mrs Dobson.

'You smell a good deal worse than you can imagine. You turned my cheese green last week, and made Mrs Hill's baby cry for two hours without stopping when she left a window open by mistake. Oh, yes, you smell badly, Kippernose, as badly as anything could smell in this world.'

'If I do all you say, if I get all neat and clean, will you stop running away and be friends?' said Kippernose.

'Of course we will,' said Jim Surtees. 'We have nothing against giants. They can be useful as long as they look where they're putting their feet and they do say the giants were the best story-tellers in the old days.'

'Just you wait and see,' shouted Kippernose. As soon as he had filled his shopping basket, he walked purposefully off towards the hills. In his basket were one hundred and twenty bars of soap, and fifty bottles of bubblebath!

That night Kippernose was busy as never before. Fires roared and hot water gurgled in all the pipes of his house. There was such a steaming, and a splashing, and a gasping, and a bubbling, and a lathering, and a singing, and a laughing, as had not been heard in Kippernose's house for a hundred years. The smell of soap and bubblebath drifted out upon the air, and as far away as the town, people caught a whiff of it.

'What's that lovely smell?' said Mrs Dobson to her husband. 'It's so beautifully clean and scented that it makes me think of a summer garden, even though it is the middle of winter.'

Next, there was a bonfire of dirty old clothes in a field near Kippernose's farm and a snip-snipping of hair and whiskers. Then there was a great rummaging in drawers and cupboards, and a shaking and airing of fresh clothes. The whole of that week, Kippernose was busy, so busy that he almost forgot to sleep and eat.

When Friday came round again, the people of the town saw an astonishing sight. Dressed in a neat Sunday suit, clean and clipped, shining in the wintry sun, and smelling of soap and sweet lavender, Kippernose strode towards them. He was a new Kippernose. The people crowded round him and Jim Surtees shouted, 'Is it really you, Kippernose?'

'It certainly *is*,' said Kippernose, beaming joyously.

'Then you're welcome amongst us,' said Jim. 'You smell as sweetly as a flower, indeed you do, and I never thought you'd do it. Three cheers for good old Kippernose! Hip. Hip.'

And the crowd cheered, 'Hooray! Hooray! Hooray!'

Kippernose was never short of friends after that. He was so good and kind that all the people

loved him and he became the happiest giant in all the world.

From that day on, if any children refused to bath, or wash, or brush their teeth, or have their hair cut, their mothers would tell them the story of Giant Kippernose.

Two

Old Man Rustytoes

There was a farmer who lived in a good country of rich and easy land and it was bad luck to his neighbours when he died, for he was the best farmer, and his was the best farm, in all those parts.

'Who will buy the farm, now Grimble's gone?' they said. 'For no one will be able to make it thrive as he did.'

None of his neighbours had the money to buy it, so the farm went to a stranger. They were all keen to see what kind of a man the new owner would be, but not a soul saw him arrive. He came at the dead of night, with his great cart rumbling along the lane, disturbing people in their sleep. But the word soon went round.

'The new man's come to Grimble's Farm. No one saw his coming. They say he came by night. There's a strange thing.' There was a shaking of heads and worried faces everywhere but for some days no one had a sight of him. There was smoke from the chimneys and a sound of hammering at Grimble's farm. There were strange roars and rumblings, but no sign of man or beast in the lanes or fields. Until the postman knocked on Farmer Rice's door on Friday morning; 'Good morning, Farmer Rice. And how do you like your new neighbour?'

'I cannot tell you that, Billy, for I haven't seen him yet,' said Farmer Rice, crossly. 'I don't even know his name. What kind of a neighbour is that? He'll come round soon enough when he wants to borrow a thresher.'

'As to his name,' said Billy, 'I can tell you that. I've just taken him a letter. He's called Garlick Rustytoes!'

'Garlick Rustytoes?' said Farmer Rice. 'What sort of a name is that? Not an honest one. Certainly not a name of our valley. Perhaps he's from the mountains, or beyond?'

'I cannot say,' said Billy, 'but his name isn't the worst thing about him.'

'Well, tell us what *is* the worst thing,' said Mrs Rice. 'If this outlandish fellow's to live near us we'd better know his worst; his best will be no hardship to find out for ourselves. Now sit down, Billy, and tell us what you know.'

'Outlandish is right,' said Billy. 'Aye, that's the word. *Outlandish*. Right well outlandish! Well. . . I'm walking into the yard with this letter for him, when I hears this awful loud snorting and gurgling coming out of the barn. Something like an elephant snoring, it was. Then I creeps nearer, and I nearly falls over myself for simple fright. Sticking out of the barn, there's this pair of feet.'

'There's nothing frightening about a pair of feet, Billy,' said Farmer Rice.

'There was about *this* pair of feet,' said Billy. 'I've not told you their size. You see, they were the size of your kitchen table! And they were on the end of legs as thick as a tree! And I'm standing there, trying to believe the truth of what I can see, when the toes begin to wriggle. I didn't wait to see more. I threw the letter on the ground and ran for it.'

'But, Billy, be sensible,' said Farmer Rice, patiently. 'Our kitchen table is four feet long. You couldn't have seen feet that size.'

'I could, and I did. Not ten minutes ago,' said Billy, indignantly.

'But if those feet were that size . . .' said Mrs Rice.

'How big would the man be on the other end of them?' demanded Farmer Rice. 'Are you trying to tell us. . .'

'I'm only telling you what I saw,' Billy grumbled.

'But a man with feet so big would be anything up to twenty feet tall!' cried Mrs Rice.

'Are you trying to tell us we have a *giant* for our new neighbour?' asked Farmer Rice.

'Make what you can of it,' said Billy, 'but I swear I'm telling you the truth of what I saw.'

'We cannot have giants living about here,' said Farmer Rice. 'This is a peaceful valley. Oh, it's different in those mountainous places. All sorts of things go on there, but it's five hundred years or more since giants were known in these parts. We're too settled and comfortable now for such goings on – and on the next farm, too. No, Billy, you must have been dreaming. You must have been.'

'My granny used to say. . .' began Mrs Rice.

'She was another dreamer,' retorted Farmer Rice.

'You'll see for yourself soon enough,' said Billy. 'I must get on with my letters or I'll never be finished today.' And off he went.

What Farmer Rice didn't see was a huge hairy arm coming over the hedge and a great hand picking up his best cow and whisking it away. Three more cows disappeared in the same way before dinner time. Poor bewildered creatures, they found themselves in a new home, with a fearsome master. Garlick Rustytoes had stolen them. When it came to milking-time, there was a great to-do. The cow-man came running, shouting, 'Master, master, four of our beasts are gone.'

'Gone? Gone? What do you mean, man, they

can't be gone. We have the best hedges and fences in the valley. There's no way my beasts could be gone,' shouted Farmer Rice.

'But they are, master, come and see!'

So they went together, all round the farm. There was no gap in hedge or fence. No gate was open. They counted the cows again, and yet again. They even brought Mrs Rice to count them. There was no mistaking it – four were missing, and the best milkers, too.

'Whoever could have taken them, knew what he was about,' moaned Farmer Rice.

'But all your gates are locked,' said Mrs Rice. 'There's no way they could have been taken, unless. . . unless. . .' She looked in the direction of Rustytoes' Farm.

'Unless *what*, woman. What do you mean to say?' cried Farmer Rice.

'Well, if that postman were right. I mean if this Rustytoes *is* a giant. . .' said Mrs Rice.

'Oh, I'll not believe such tales,' Farmer Rice snapped, and stamped out of the house.

At all the farms bordering Rustytoes land, strange things began to happen.

Ten sheep disappeared at Apple Tree Farm. A horse and three pigs vanished from Hill Top Farm. A hut full of hens was whisked away at night at Mill Farm, so swiftly and smoothly that not a single hen wakened on its roost to give a warning. Farmer Rice even lost a barn and all the hay and oats in it, from an outlying field. There was only a pale square of grass to show where it had been!

'Now what did I tell you?' said Mrs Rice. 'There's only one sort of person could do a thing like that, and that's. . .'

'Now I'll not have you frightening people with talk of giants,' grumbled Farmer Rice. 'There are lots of ways these things could happen. Have you never heard of gypsies and rogues and vagabonds? They did a lot of mischief in the old days. Who knows but they may have come back again.'

'Gypsies, indeed,' snorted Mrs Rice, but she said no more, seeing the mood her husband was in. She attacked her pastry with the rolling pin, as if to say, 'That's for your gypsies!'

But things only got worse. Heavy footsteps shook the country roads by night and things began to disappear from more distant farms, up and down the valley. A plough and a cart disappeared as far away as Windmill Farm. Mysterious shadows fell across bedroom windows in the moonlight and people trembled in their beds. Though the dogs barked, no one dared to go out to see what was stirring. The whole valley was afraid, and no one knew what to do. Until the postman called again at Rice's

Farm, and Farmer Rice had an idea.

'Pass the word round, Billy,' he said, 'to every farm you visit. Tell every farmer who has had anything stolen to meet on Crompton village green at ten o'clock on Wednesday morning. Then we'll all visit Rustytoes. We'll have to get to the bottom of this and I can think of no other way.'

'That I will,' said Billy. 'It's the best idea I've heard yet.' And off he went, to carry his message about the valley.

Billy did his work well. At ten o'clock on Wednesday morning there was a large and angry crowd of farmers on Crompton Green. There was a man from almost every farm for ten miles around. Each one carried a pitchfork or a stout stick.

'Friends,' shouted Farmer Rice. 'You all know why we're here, don't you?'

'Aye, we do,' murmured the farmers.

'Every man here has had stock and machinery stolen in the last two weeks,' went on Farmer Rice, 'and no ordinary thief could carry off cows in broad daylight, with no sight or sound of their going. Besides, we're honest folks in this valley. There's been no thieving here for hundreds of years. But we have a new neighbour – this Garlick Rustytoes; and I cannot help noticing that his fields are suddenly full of cattle and sheep, when he's not once been to market since he came here. Indeed, nobody has so much as seen his face. So, men, I suggest we all pay a call on our new neighbour, and ask him a few questions!'

'But, Farmer Rice,' called Jim Dobson, 'some say this Rustytoes is nothing less than a giant!'

'There's no need to upset people with wild talk of giants,' said Farmer Rice. 'Nobody's set eyes on the fellow yet, so how can anyone say?'

Luckily for Farmer Rice, Billy was away with his letters, for his story of Rustytoes' enormous feet could have scared even these angry men away.

'To Rustytoes' Farm, then!' shouted Farmer Rice. 'Come on, let's rouse him!' And he led

the way with the buzzing mob of farmers
following, their staves and pitchforks jaunting at
the ready.

There seemed to be no one about at Rustytoes'
Farm, but as they approached the house the
farmers grew more and more excited, as they
spied their stolen property. Cries went up on all

sides: 'There's my sheep! There's my Daisy and her two calves! Bless me, there's my barn, and all the hay still in it! So that's where my thresher went to!' And so on, all the way up to Rustytoes' door. By then they were so angry that they hammered on the door fit to break it down.

'Come out, you thief!' they shouted. 'We've come for our property! It's no good hiding; we've got eyes to see. Come on, hand it all over!'

Some looked in the windows, but couldn't see anyone. Then, a thunderous voice boomed out of the sky at them, 'What, little midgets, do you dare to come and trouble Rustytoes?'

They all looked upwards. A great grinning face loomed above them. Rustytoes was leaning on the farmhouse roof as though it were a low gate, and leering over at them.

'I'll take what I want, and none can stop me, so take yourselves off before I squash you!' he roared. Then he came stamping round the house to show his full height. Not one man stayed to argue. You cannot argue with an angry giant, for that is what he truly was, twenty or thirty feet high. They all scampered off as fast as they could go, with Rustytoes' laughter bellowing after them.

They didn't stop until they reached Crompton Green again, then every man flopped on to the grass to get his breath back.

'What are we going to do?' moaned Farmer Rice. 'Billy was right; Rustytoes *is* a giant. I was right, and he *has* stolen our things, and means to go on stealing. But we cannot send a giant to prison and we cannot fight him. What can we do?'

'He'll take what he wants until we're all too poor to go on farming,' said Jim Dobson gloomily. 'He'll take our land next and we'll have to go and live in the mountains.'

'Oh, it cannot be as bad as that, surely,' said Farmer Rice, but he couldn't convince even himself. They all fell into a gloomy silence and drifted off home one by one.

Things did get worse, much worse. Rustytoes took what he wanted and the farmers of the valley grew poorer and poorer. Rustytoes was so big and strong that no one could stop him.

Soon Rustytoes began to make the other farmers do all his work, too. He had his bed in the big barn and he lay there all day, eating sweets. He lay on the straw, laughing at the little men as they hurried about to do his work. Rustytoes grew rich and fat and lazy, but he was as strong as ever, and everyone feared him.

'Can you not think of a way of overcoming this Rustytoes?' Mrs Rice demanded of her husband.

'I can not,' said Farmer Rice. 'He's just too big and strong to be defied.'

'Then what will become of us,' moaned Mrs Rice.

'I cannot tell, my dear, but it's a black outlook,' said Farmer Rice, and went gloomily off to bed.

But something did overcome Garlick Rustytoes. Something quite simple. Something natural.

One morning, the neighbourhood woke to a strange sound. A roaring, moaning, bellowing sound, that came and went with the wind, and sighed amongst the trees. There it was again, louder.

'What in the world is that?' exclaimed Mrs Rice at breakfast.

'Bless me, I don't know,' said Farmer Rice. They went outside to listen.

A yowling and howling echoed across the fields.

'What a dreadful noise,' said Farmer Rice. 'It will turn the milk sour.'

'It's coming from Rustytoes' Farm,' said Mrs Rice.

'It's some new trick of his,' said Farmer Rice.

'No, it sounds like someone in pain,' said Mrs Rice. 'Come on, we must go and see. It sounds so pitiful.'

So they crept up to Rustytoes' farm and fearfully approached the big barn, from where all the noise seemed to be coming. Great roars and yells, low moans growing to a sound like thunder, thumpings and gaspings, sighing and weeping, came from the open door. Rustytoes' feet, sticking out, thrashed about. Trembling, Farmer Rice and his wife looked in. There was poor Rustytoes, lying on the straw with the side of his face all swollen.

'Oh, help me, please help me,' he moaned, seeing them.

'Why, you great fellow, what's happened to you?' asked the astonished Mrs Rice, who had never seen him before.

'*Toothache*. I've got toothache,' moaned Rustytoes. 'Oooooooh, and it does hurt.'

'A giant toothache, too,' said Mrs Rice. 'The pain's as big as he is and it must be dreadful. It's laid him low, great as he is. Poor fellow, he has an abscess on that tooth the size of a cow and nothing hurts more.'

'But he's bad, and he's a giant, and it serves him right,' whispered Farmer Rice.

'Bad he may be, but we must help him. You cannot let anyone suffer so, and not help,' protested Mrs Rice. To Rustytoes she said, 'Now lie still, and I'll make you a poultice, and I'll gather some herbs that will ease your pain. Then

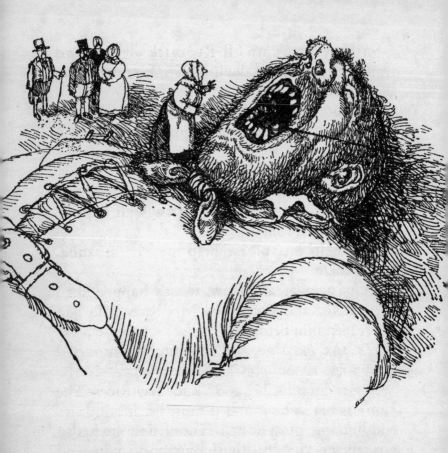

we'll bring the dentist from the village and see if he can get that tooth out of you.'

'You're a kind woman, Mrs Rice,' said Rustytoes, groaning between his words. 'Oooh! Owch! If you help me, I'll promise to be good and kind to you and all the farmers. Oooh! I cannot bear the pain. I've been awake all night with it. It's too much for me. I'll die if you don't take this pain away! I'll give back all that I've stolen, if only you'll help me. *Please* help me, good people.'

'Do you *promise*?' said Farmer Rice. 'Do you promise to give back all that you have stolen? Everything?'

'Yes. Yes. Everything.'

'Do you promise to be good to all your neighbours, and never steal or frighten anyone again?'

'Yes. I promise. All you say,' moaned Rustytoes. 'Anything to be rid of this pain.'

'Then we'll do all we can to make you better,' declared Farmer Rice.

'Oh, stop your talking, and let's see to the poor fellow,' said Mrs Rice, and she got to work.

Never was there such a busy scene. More people arrived and Mrs Rice set them to work. The women gathered herbs, and made a giant poultice with two sheets. Farmer Rice excitedly told all the farmers about Rustytoes' promises. The dentist was sent for and he climbed bravely into Rustytoes' mouth to examine the bad tooth. He came out looking dazed saying the tooth was the size of a loaf and that it would have to come out. A big rope-sling was made, to pull the tooth. Ten horses were brought and harnessed to a long rope fastened to the sling. And all the time, Rustytoes moaned on, though Mrs Rice's

herbs had soothed his pains. At last, all was
ready. The sling was round the tooth and the
horses ready to pull.

'Take the strain!' called Farmer Rice. The ropes
tightened as the horses tensed their muscles.

'Pull!' shouted Farmer Rice, and all the men
urged their horses on.

'Heave! Come on, my beauty! Pull, my girl!
Come on, now!' So they coaxed on them and the
horses pulled with all their strength. The ropes
creaked and cracked with the great strain. All
eyes were on the tooth. It didn't move. More

horses were brought – fifteen, then twenty. They all pulled again and the great tooth moved slightly. Then the men took the ropes, and pulled with the horses.

'All together!' called Farmer Rice. 'One. Two. Three, and pull.' Horses and men pulled and pulled with all their strength. There was a loud crack. The tooth shot out releasing the rope, so that the horses galloped off down the lane and everyone fell over in a heap. Amid all the noise and muddle, there was Rustytoes, sitting up and smiling all over his face.

'It's gone!' he exclaimed. 'It's gone. Oh, what a wonderful feeling.' They all looked at him. 'What good people you are,' he said. 'I've been as bad as I could be to you and yet you all come to help me when I'm in pain.'

'But you made us some promises,' Farmer Rice reminded him.

'And I'll keep them,' said Rustytoes, happily. 'Better than that, I'll be the best neighbour you ever had, from this day on. I'll help you with your work, and protect you from your enemies. Whatever you want, I'm your giant; at your service, good friends.'

Rustytoes kept his word. He gave everything back. He worked hard to help anyone who asked him. He moved barns and uprooted trees. He dug new roads and dammed a river. He helped to build houses and farms. No one ever dared to attack the people of the valley, with a giant to defend them, so there was peace as never before. The people of the valley became happy and prosperous and they grew very fond of their giant. Everyone knew him as Dear Old Man Rustytoes and they all loved and trusted him. Even so, Farmer Rice kept an eye on him.

'You can never be sure, with giants,' he said.

'Never fear,' said Mrs Rice. 'Old Man Rustytoes has a great many more teeth in his head, and he might need another one pulling, one of these days.'

Three

The giant who swallowed the wind

Once there was a giant. He lived in a land of many winds, where windmills ground the corn and pumped the water. He was a hungry giant. He was always hungry. He would stride across the fields and his voice would roll about the hills like thunder, bellowing, 'Little men! Do you hear me? I'm hungry. Bring me flour. Bring me sheep and pigs and good fat cows. Bring me cheese and butter and milk. Bring me sweets and cakes and ice-cream. I'm so hungry!'

The people were very frightened of him so they gave him all he wanted. The millers gave him flour by the cart-load. The farmers gave him whole herds of sheep and cows, whole litters of fat squealing pigs, and buckets full of milk. The good wives baked him great baskets full of cakes, and made him enormous cheeses and tubs of butter. They filled their babies' bath-tubs full of ice-cream for him. The children saved all their sweets for him and had none left for themselves.

They all said, 'If we keep the giant full of food he will do us no harm; we can sleep safely in our beds and fear nothing.'

That greedy giant would put all this food into a capacious sack and carry it off to his hill. Then he would sit on his hill and stuff and stuff for a whole week. Then he would sleep for a week and sing for a week. Then he would take a walk by the sea. Then he would come back for more! Oh, how the people wearied of him with his never-satisfied hunger.

'We will never grow rich and comfortable,' they said, 'with such an insatiable giant to feed. He cannot ever be filled, and bless us all, he is surely *growing*. His hunger will grow too!' It did. Month by month he demanded, 'More! Give me more! I'm more hungry than ever.' And his sack bulged larger and larger.

One day young Bob Miller said to his father, 'Do you know, Dad, I don't believe that giant would do us any harm if we stopped feeding him.'

'Stop feeding him? Stop feeding him? What are you saying, son? Have you gone out of your wits?' said old Robert Miller.

'I've just found them,' said young Bob. 'That giant has never said that he would harm us if we gave him no food. He has always shouted for food and we have always given it to him because he shouted. He has never hurt anyone.'

'That's true,' said his mother; 'my granny used to say the giant played with the children when she was a girl. That was before he grew too big to live in a house and went to live on that hill of his.'

'And haven't you heard him singing?' cried Bob. 'I have crept by his hill on many a summer day, and heard him outsing the birds of the air. A giant who sings so cheerfully cannot really be bad.'

'I believe you have it, boy,' said old Robert, leaping to his feet. 'We'll try him out. Next time he comes there will be no food for him. Then we'll see!'

The word went quickly round. People whispered, one to another, '*No food for the giant. No food? Gracious me. What will become of us? But Robert Miller says it will be all right. You'll see.*'

Now Robert Miller was known everywhere as the wisest man in the land. Everyone trusted him. So, after some arguments with the fearful and difficult folks among them, all the people agreed. There would be no food for the giant next time he came.

Thump, thump, thump, thump, thump, came the giant's heavy tread across the fields. His voice rumbled thunderously about the hills and shook

the ragged rooks out of their nests.

'Little men! Do you hear me? I'm hungry, oh so hungry. Bring me food. More food. My hunger grows upon me.'

Mothers and children hid under beds and in cellars. A brave but trembling group of millers and farmers stood in a wind-blown field, stoutly facing the giant. Robert Miller stood on a barrel and shouted with all his might, 'Go away! We have nothing for you. No food. We need it all for ourselves and our hungry wives and children. Now what do you say to that?'

'No food?' rumbled the giant, in mountainous surprise. 'But I'm hungry. I'm hungry, I tell you, and you've always given me food. You've got to give me food.'

'Oh no we haven't, and we're not going to give you anymore, ever,' shouted Robert and all the men cheered.

'I could stamp your houses down and smash your windmills,' said the giant, trying to look fierce.

'If you did that we wouldn't be able to grow any more food for you, or grind your flour,' pointed out Robert.

'True,' said the giant, then he stamped his feet in the field anyway, because he was so cross. The ground shook so alarmingly that almost half the men were ready to give in to him, but not tough old Robert.

'Would you want to kill poor helpless people; mothers and babies with their houses crushed on top of them?' he shouted to the giant.

'Certainly not,' said the giant and looked ashamed. He hid his head in some low clouds and rumbled to himself for a while, then he stumped away to his hill without another word.

But they had not won. Not a bit of it. The giant was not going to give in so easily. He had thought of a trick to play on the little men. He strode home across the fields, and climbed to the top of his hill. It was the highest hill in the country and no wind could miss it. There, he stood with all the winds of the land blowing about him. He puffed all the breath out of his enormous lungs. Then, opening his mouth wide, he sucked and sucked and sucked mightily. There was a moaning and a rushing and a whooshing. From every direction the winds came, and the giant's great mouth sucked them all in, and they whirled and swirled deep, deep down into his great body. Not even the smallest breeze escaped. All the winds disappeared into that terribly hungry giant. Then he closed his mouth tightly, lay down, and went to sleep. The winds rumbled about deep inside him and gave him bad dreams, but they couldn't get out.

The giant had swallowed the wind.

Now that there was no wind in all the land, every single windmill stopped. No corn could be ground into flour, so the bakers could not bake any bread. No water could be pumped, so the fields began to flood and all the farmers' crops began to spoil. The cows and sheep could not crop the flooded grass and they grew thinner and thinner.

'Where have all the winds gone?' moaned the people, as starvation came daily nearer. Until one day, when Bob Miller went far afield seeking rabbits for the pot. He came home in great excitement.

'I know where the winds have gone!' he cried. 'I went close by the giant's hill, and I heard the wind blowing and swooshing, sighing and moaning, in the queerest way, as though it were trapped in a big old chimney with a feather pillow stuffed in the top. Then I guessed. The wind was inside the giant! It was grumbling round, looking for a way out. He must have swallowed all our winds, the old trickster.'

'This is his revenge on us,' wailed Bob's mother. 'I feared he was up to some mischief. What is to become of us? We will all starve.'

'Shush, mother, you'll frighten the nation with your wailing. Now I have a plan to outwit the giant, but it must be a secret even from you. Dear mother, will you promise to be quiet a while and say nothing of all this?'

'Very well, son, I know what a clever lad you are. But don't be putting yourself in any danger, now, will you?'

'I'll be safe enough,' said Bob, though he was not at all sure that he would be.

That night, when all were asleep and the moon was bright, Bob dressed and silently crept out of the mill. He went to the hut where the geese were sleeping and took the three longest and fluffiest feathers he could find. Then he walked along dark lanes and hedgerows clear of the floods, until he reached the giant's hill. The giant slept uneasily on, the winds still racing about within him. Bob climbed right up to him. Then he took off his shoes and began to climb the mountainous sides of the giant himself. Up his leg and across his heaving stomach went Bob; across the great chest to the jutting cliff of the giant's chin. Digging his toes into the giant's beard, Bob hauled himself up until he was sitting on his chin. Taking the feathers from his belt, Bob strode across that fearsome mouth until he stood in the shadowed cave of the giant's left nostril. Shaking with fear, Bob thrust the feathers as far into the giant's nose as he could, sweeping them round and round the nostrils' walls. It was the biggest tickle that ever was! It was too much, even for a giant: his nose began to quiver, he took a deep breath, and, 'Aaaaaaaaaaaaaaaaaaaaa tiSHOOOO!' he sneezed a sneeze that shook the world. It was like ten gales, a hurricane and a tornado all at once. And with the sneeze, out came all the winds that the giant had swallowed; they spread at once all over the land, setting the windmills whirling. Bob, too, was blown out with the sneeze. He was blown high and far above the clouds, and he came down with a jolt, half an hour later, right outside his own front door. It was morning by then, and all the people were at their doors rubbing their eyes at the sight of the windmills working again.

When Bob dropped out of the clouds, his mother cried, 'Gracious, son, where have you been and what have you done with your shoes?'

'Never mind my shoes, mother,' grinned Bob, 'I've brought something better than an old pair of shoes.'

'You've brought the wind, the lovely wind,' sang his father; 'we're all saved. You're a hero!'

When Bob told all his story, the people cheered and heaped presents upon him. Everyone rejoiced. The windmills were working again. The water could be pumped from the fields and the crops were saved. The corn could be ground and

the bread baked. Better still, the giant admitted that he had been outwitted. He was too ashamed to show his face again and went away to live by the sea in a desolate place where no men lived. He would wade far out to sea and catch dolphins and seals and, sometimes, a whale.

With no giant to pester them, the people were more happy and prosperous than they had ever been. There was food enough for all and the

children could keep their sweets for themselves. If there was any food to spare, it was sent as a present to the giant, just to show there was no hard feeling. And the wives cooked him a pudding every Christmas.

Bob Miller never did find his shoes. Goodness knows where *they* were blown to.

Four

The sleeping giant

Once there was a giant who lived in Sussex. It was a long time ago; so long ago that there were no men at all in that part of the world. So it was pleasant and peaceful for the giant, living on the low green hills, not far from the sea. Quietly he lived there for hundreds of years. The sea cooled him in the heat of the summer; the Downs sheltered him from the cold winter winds. Then a time came when a great tiredness grew upon him; he had lived so long that he had become weary of the world. Now when this mood came upon a giant, the best thing for him to do was to have a long, long sleep. He would sleep for a hundred years, two hundred years, perhaps even as long as a thousand years. When he woke up the world would be new again, and life sweet. This is just what the Sussex giant decided to do. He lay down among the Sussex Downs and went into his long sleep.

Now if you have seen the Sussex Downs, you will know that they are long hills, rounded on top and at the ends; not unlike the shape of a sleeping giant, covered with an eiderdown. There, among these hills, this giant slept, and he didn't stir for centuries. Summer and winter passed over him again and again, times beyond counting. The leaves of autumn drifted over him, and rotted down into a rich humus. The winds of winter blew loose soil over him and heaped it against his sides. The birds dropped twigs and seeds upon him and built their nests in

his hair. The giant lay quite still. Grass and flowers began to grow upon him, and slowly they covered him. Where the earth was deeply piled, trees began to grow. Not knowing, not caring, the giant slept on. And as time passed he came to look more and more like the hills he slept among, and a time came when sharp-nosed foxes hunted the length of him without knowing there was any giant there at all.

Long years passed, and still the giant slept on; and at last men came to live in Sussex, bringing

their wives and children, their cows, and sheep and pigs. They lived on the rich plain of the Weald. They lived by the sea. They lived on the gentle slopes of the Downs. Without knowing it, they lived on the giant himself. How could they know? There was no sign to tell them that this particular sunny hillside was anything more than just a sunny hillside, made of chalk and flint. There was nothing to tell them that under the grass and flowers, under the owl-haunted trees, a giant was sleeping his long, long sleep. So they lived happily on the giant.

They built farms and homesteads on him. They cleared the land and planted fields of wheat and barley on his chest and stomach. They built a windmill on his head. Paths and bridleways and roads crossed the giant in all directions. Cows grazed on the length of his legs and on the slopes of his sides; his arms and shoulders bore sheep in great flocks. Generations of children were born on the giant, and grew up on him, and passed their whole lives on him, without ever knowing the giant was there under their feet all the time. And still the giant slept tranquilly on, year after year.

Then a year came when there was a terrible drought. Week after week there was not so much as a drop of rain; men and beasts grew desperate with thirst and the earth was baked hard by the flailing heat of the sun. There never was much water on the Downs, and the people had to collect what they could from dew-ponds and rainbarrels. Now the dew-ponds dried up and the barrels were almost empty. A little water could be brought from the river in the plain, but it was a long and dangerous journey, and it was not enough for their needs. Week after week the sun flamed in the sky and still no wisp of cloud appeared. All living creatures gasped for life and the farmers faced ruin. It was then that George Bonyface decided to dig a well. George had farmed on the giant Down for twenty years, but no one had ever thought of digging a well in all that time.

'A well?' said his wife, Sarah. 'A well? You must be out of your wits! You know yourself that wells are no good on these Downland farms; everybody says so.'

'*Who* says so?' scowled George.

'Everybody!' declared Sarah, banging her pans.

'And has everybody tried digging a well?' demanded George.

'They don't need to,' said Sarah. 'They know it would be a waste of time. Come to think of it, there was a fellow over by Chanctonbury that my old grandfather knew years and years ago. He dug a well. He had ten men digging for two weeks, and they found nothing but chalk and flint; not a drop of water. And a cow fell into the hole, before they could fill it in, and broke its poor neck; the best cow they had, too. That farm never came to any good after that.'

'But all our cows will die of thirst if we don't find water somehow and then what will become of us?' protested George. 'It's our last chance, and it's worth a try. Chanctonbury's a long way from here and no one's ever tried digging a well on our hill. It might be different from all the other Downs. Who knows, it might be full of water!'

'There's no telling you,' sighed Sarah.

'Just you wait and see,' said George. 'I have a feeling about this hill. I'm sure there's *something* under the ground. It's different from the other Downs. There's something about the rise and fall of its slopes; the feel of it when you're ploughing. Just you wait and see.'

Early the next day, George gathered all his men together. He explained what he wanted them to do and picked a spot most carefully, in a little dip in the ground, where he thought water would be most likely to collect. They struck their picks and shovels into the ground, and a deepening hole soon bit into the parched earth. Down and down they dug. Below the sun-baked crust the ground was softer and slightly moist and the digging easier. Down and down they dug, throwing up a growing pile of chalk. By dinner-time the diggers' heads were out of sight. A crowd of watchers had gathered curiously round, some jeering, some hopeful. They jostled each other to peer into the hole, each hoping to be the first to see water seeping under the weary diggers' feet. But there was no sign of water when George called a halt for dinner. The men grumbled that they were wasting their time and George had to offer them double pay to go on. They shuffled away wearily to their homes, leaving George to stare dolefully into his dry hole, a nudging crowd at his back.

'Just you wait and see!' he shouted. 'We haven't gone deep enough yet.' And he leaped into the hole, took up a spade, and began to dig. Within five minutes his spade met something it could not bite into. Down on his knees, George brushed the loose chalk clear with his hands, and looked amazed at what lay under him.

'What is it?' called Tom Miller. 'What have you found, George? Is it water, at last?'

'Not water,' said George, his voice coming booming out of the hole. 'You'll think this daft, I know, but it looks like a layer of rough cloth! Come and see for yourself.'

Tom Miller climbed down into the hole and knelt by George. Together they felt all about the hole's floor.

'Right enough,' said Tom. 'It does feel like very

rough cloth and it goes right under the rock; there's no break in it at all. Let's dig sideways to see if we can find the edge of it.'

With pick and spade they dug carefully, extending the hole on each side, making a kind of underground cave.

'There's no end to it,' exclaimed George.

'Right enough,' said Tom. 'It goes on under the ground; we'll not find an edge to it. We'll have to cut through it. Try that pick on it. It's got a sharp enough point.'

George took up the pick, and struck it hard into the rough cloth. The point pricked through into what lay below. The point pricked through into the giant's skin! Again and again George brought the point of his pick down on to that tough, tough cloth. Again and again, without guessing it, he pricked and pricked the skin of the sleeping giant's tummy. Deep in his dreams the giant felt a sharp pain, pricking and pricking at him. Deep in his sleep of centuries, the giant began to stir. The pain would not let him rest. It nagged on and on, pricking and pricking at him. Slowly, and slowly, the giant began to waken. After hundreds and hundreds of years of sleep, a giant's wakening is a slow and gentle affair; but George's pick went on and on, pricking and prodding the giant into wakefulness. The giant groaned.

'Is that thunder?' said Tom.

'There's a storm brewing,' said George. 'We shall have rain, anyway.'

'More like an earthquake,' said Tom. 'I'm sure I felt the ground shaking.'

The giant stirred in his wakening.

'The ground's moving!' yelled George. 'Run for it! It's an earthquake!'

All the people standing round the hole scattered and frightened faces appeared at cottage doors. Tom and George scrambled out of the hole, flinging down pick and spade, and ran for their homes. Too late! The giant was wakening now. Again he stirred and soil and rocks fell from his sides. Coming slowly out of his sleep, he stretched and tried all his muscles. He wiggled his toes, and a cottage went sliding down into the valley. The ground shook and trembled more and more violently The windmill toppled over and rolled thumping into the valley.

'Run! Run!' shouted George. 'Run down to the valleys for safety! It's an earthquake!'

All the people ran away from the giant Down as fast as they could. They knocked on the doors of fearful farmers in the valley and scurried to hide with them in cellars and under beds. And all this time the giant was wakening up. He felt the soil and rocks lying on him and could not think what it was. He felt the cows and sheep

running about on him, and thought it might be fleas. So he shook himself and scratched himself, and trees, and rocks, and grass, and flowers, and cows, and sheep, and pigs, all went slipping and sliding and showering down his sides, to be tumbled all in a heap in the valley below. He gave himself a great shake, and farms and cottages tumbled down. He brushed them away like so much dust. Slowly, the giant sat up. He scratched at his stomach where George Bonyface had pricked him and wondered who could have

made that little hole in his trousers. He gazed about at the changed countryside, and smiled happily, for the world was made anew for him. He stood up, and yawned widely, a yawn that sounded like dreadful thunder to the men shivering in cellars and under beds. He stretched and stamped, making the earth quiver for fifty miles around. He laughed at the sun and the wind in his face. He felt so wonderful after his long sleep, that he thought he must travel about and see more of the world. One great stride took him to the sea-shore; another took him far out to sea. He was so big that the sea only came up to his knees. So away he went, striding across the glittering sea, and on and on, becoming smaller and smaller with distance; dipping away below the horizon, and was gone.

All was silent and still in Sussex, and in the place where the giant had lain, there was a new valley, full of tumbled carts and stones. One by one, the people came out of the places where they had been hiding and stared in wonder at the place where their Downland hill had been.

'Water!' cried Sarah Bonyface. 'We have found water after all. Look!'

A spring of clear water poured from the new valley slope, and a shining thread of water ran the length of the new valley to join the distant River Ouse.

'What a way to dig a well,' smiled George. 'We'll never go thirsty again, that's for sure.'

'But our houses?' said Sarah. 'Where have they gone?'

'The earthquake shook them down when it made the new valley. Never fear, we'll build them up again, better than they were before. It's good riddance to that windy old hill, I say. Now we have a sunny and sheltered valley, with good southerly slopes; we'll be able to grow raspberries and strawberries, now; plums and pears and sweet apples. We'll be better off than ever we were on that old hill, you'll see.'

George was right. New farms and cottages were soon built and the valley became the richest and happiest place in all Sussex. No one knew they had a giant to thank for all their good fortune, for not one person had seen the giant rise up and stride away. As for George Bonyface, he became famous as the champion well-digger of all time.

Five

The story of Giant Bogweed

There was once a giant who lived in a wild part of Yorkshire, and a right nasty fellow he was too. He lived on the desolate moors away beyond Malham, and he was sour and bad tempered and murderously strong, and he did all he could to cause trouble and distress to the people who lived in those parts. Everybody was terrified of him, but it was worst for the farmers because he stole their sheep and cattle for food, and knocked their barns and byres down out of sheer bad temper. He suffered aches and cramps from living on the damp moors, and when the pains were upon him he would groan and bellow enough to frighten the very birds of the air. It was at such times that he played his nastiest tricks. He set fire to all Jim Hargreaves' haystacks once. He uprooted a dozen trees and piled them in the main road to block it, and it took the village men a month of hard work to shift them. He was so strong and big that no one could stop him doing just as he pleased and he was hated and feared throughout the country; as far away as Hawes and Skipton, folks trembled at the mention of his name.

His name suited him. They called him Giant Bogweed. The stink and slime of the moorland bogs were never far from him; the bogs that were foul and treacherous, like Giant Bogweed himself: And when children were naughty, mothers and grannies would say, 'Hush! Hush! Giant Bogweed comes for bad children. Hush your crying or he'll hear you – Giant Bogweed will come down from the moors and get you!'

And even the naughtiest of children would lie quiet and go to sleep.

Every spring, the farmers of Malham drove their flocks up the steep moorland roads to their summer pastures, high above the village. The sheep scattered for miles across the stony moors, cropping the tough grasses. This was a time that the farmers and shepherds feared, for they had to follow their sheep to the wild moors where Giant Bogweed lived and they walked in terror, for that dreadful fellow could be round every next turning in the lane, over the next hill, or wallowing in the next slimy pool. Now there was a green road that crossed the whole moor, called Mastiles Lane, and every farmer drove his sheep and cattle along it to reach the distant pastures, or to attend the fairs and markets at Conistone or Grassington. To this day it is one of the famous green roads of Yorkshire, grassy and peaceful; it is a lovely place to walk now, but at that time it was shadowed by fear because of Bogweed's lurking presence. There came a year when Bogweed was in a worse temper than ever and he decided to make life as unpleasant as he could for the farmers of Malham. One dark midnight, he tossed a large boulder into the middle of the village. It rolled along for some way, smashing some nice trees down and knocking down Granny Dryden's garden wall, until it ended up against Joe Hartley's farmhouse wall with an almighty thump. Joe ran out in his night-shirt to see what was up and so he was the first to read the message, for there was a message, written in tar on a stolen table-cloth and tied round the stone. Joe struggled to untie the cloth and spread it out under the moon's dim light. The ugly words seemed to flicker as black clouds hid the moon but they were clear enough.

'MASTILES LANE IS MINE. KEEP OFF. I WILL GOBBLE UP ANY MAN OR BEAST THAT SETS FOOT ON IT. KEEP OUT. TRESPASSERS WILL BE PERSECUTED AND EATEN. BY ORDER.

BOGWEED THE GRIM.'

The rest of the village was soon awake, and people gathered round Joe in the dark, to read the strange message. Joe kept prodding people angrily and shouting into the wind, 'Look at it! Look at it! It's that beast of a giant. He thinks he can stop us using Mastiles Lane. Says he'll gobble us up. *Gobble* us up, indeed!'

He went on like this until his wife, Elsie, called from the door, 'Joe, for goodness sake come in and get dressed, you'll catch your death!'

'Get dressed?' shouted Joe. 'I'm going back to bed. There's nothing to be done tonight. Let them all see for themselves.'

He stumped crossly to his door. Before he went in, he turned towards the group by the cloth and shouted, 'But that giant won't stop me going over Mastiles. I'm going to Grassington Fair next week and that's the way I'm going, whatever anybody says.' With that he banged his door. The little group stood bewildered by the cloth.

'I wondered where my table-cloth had gone,' grumbled Granny Dryden. 'I thought the wind had blown it off the line, but now look at it. How will I ever get all that tar off it?'

'Never mind your cloth,' said Jim Richardson. 'What about us getting to Grassington? It's near twenty miles going round by the road but it's only five or six miles over Mastiles. How can we sell our cattle if we have to go all that way?'

'And what about the pastures?' said Bob Varley. 'I can only get to mine over Mastiles. My sheep will starve if I can't take them that way. Do you think he *would* gobble us up?'

'I'm sure of it,' said Jim. 'He's gobbled plenty of my sheep over the years; he could gobble a man just as easily. It's my guess he's getting more greedy and more hungry as time goes on.'

'My poor cloth,' murmured Granny Dryden.

'Oh shut up about your old cloth,' snapped Jim. 'We have more serious things to worry about than a bit of table-cloth.'

'Let me tell you. . .' began Granny Dryden.

'Hush, now,' said Bob Varley, 'we mustn't quarrel. Let's all go to our beds and sleep on it and talk it over calmly by the light of day.'

So they all grumbled off to their beds.

The next morning a new crowd collected round Giant Bogweed's message, a bigger crowd, with excited children and tattling women added to the angry groups of farmers and their men. All morning, people kept on coming to see the message, and people visiting the village were all brought to see it. The story of Giant Bogweed's evil message soon spread far about the Yorkshire Dales.

Then, at tea-time, Granny Dryden came out and said, 'Well it's my cloth, anyway.'

And she snatched it up and took it away; she spent several days scrubbing it and boiling it, but she couldn't get the message off, and she ended up throwing it into the fire.

In spite of this, no one could forget the nasty words, and many would remember them to the end of their days. Joe Hartley never wavered. If anyone asked him, he said, 'I'm going over Mastiles with my sheep next Friday to be at Grassington Fair; no slimy, smelly old giant's going to frighten me with his silly message.'

'But Joe, he will gobble you up, and your sheep, and then what will become of us?' wailed his wife.

'Oh, Elsie, hush your noise, no giant's going to gobble me up. I feel it in my bones. Let him have one sheep, and he'll be full for three days, and by the time he's slept it off I'll be safely home from the fair with my pockets full of money,' said Joe, smiling. Then their son, little Willie, began to cry and plead with his father, 'Oh Dad, don't go that way! Please don't go. He really is the worst giant that ever lived; everyone says so. You cannot tell what he will do if you go against him. Please don't go. I'll help you take the sheep round by the main road. I will, I don't care how far it is.'

'Well I do care how far it is. They'll all be lame by the time we get there if we go that way,' said Joe. 'Now stop it, both of you; I'm going over Mastiles and that's that.'

No one could persuade Joe Hartley not to go over Mastiles. Not one other farmer would dare go. 'All the better,' said Joe, 'I'll get better prices for my sheep.' Elsie even brought the parson to argue with him, but it was no good. 'Parson knows nothing about farming,' said Joe, when he had gone. So, early on Friday morning, Joe set out, with a large flock of sheep, to walk the length of Mastiles Lane in defiance of Giant Bogweed. He wore his best boots and carried a stout stick. All the village turned out to see him off and gave him a rousing cheer for a brave fellow. No one noticed that little Willie crept out by the back door, and followed his father at some distance, keeping out of sight behind the stone walls of the fields.

Little Willie was good at moving without being seen. He loved to watch the moorland birds and animals, so he had had good practice. When you have tracked a fox over five fields without being seen or scented, then it is easy to follow a man with a noisy flock of sheep. So Willie silently followed his father, away from the safety of the village, out on to the wild moors. The piteous bleating of the sheep was carried to him on the wind, punctuated by the busy barking of the dogs; the curlews bubbled in the clear sky; the wind ruffled the brown water in the peaty pools.

The moor seemed very big and very lonely to Willie. He longed to catch up with his father and take hold of his strong hand but this wouldn't do at all; this was not what Willie had come for. He knew, anyway, that his father would send him straight home the moment he saw him. No, Willie must keep going alone – secretly, silently.

They were two miles or more, out from the village, when Willie saw a dark shape on the horizon, close to the track, some way ahead of Joe and the flock.

'Is it Giant Bogweed? Oh, no, don't let it be,' whispered Willie agonisingly to himself. But the shape moved and it was too big for any animal. 'It is, it is, it's Bogweed, I'm sure of it.' The certainty grew upon Willie but he dare not, must not, cry out. It was too late for Joe to turn back and escape so Willie must stay hidden, escape capture, and help his father if he could. A small hill hid Bogweed from Joe. Bogweed grinned and licked his lips, and waited. Willie saw it all at a distance. The eager sheep running ahead, then stopping, astonished, at the enormous sight of Bogweed. The dogs barking and snapping furiously. Joe himself, bravely standing to fight Bogweed. Then the thunderous laughter of Bogweed rolling over the hills and Joe snatched up, kicking helplessly, and bundled into a sack tied to Bogweed's belt. Then Bogweed lashing the dogs till they whined and triumphantly driving off the whole flock away from the road, across the fields towards a dark mountain slope. Oh, how Willie had to strive to stop himself from rushing up to fight Bogweed himself, big as the brutish thing was!

'It's foolish to fight. Stay, stay and watch, and follow, then there will be hope,' he told himself. So Willie secretly followed Bogweed miles across the stony fells. He panted after him over rocky slopes. He scrambled and squelched over boggy places. Bogweed strode away at speed and it was all Willie could do to keep up. Luckily, the sheep slowed the giant down, giving Willie the chance to keep them all in sight.

So Willie followed over countless miles, until at last Bogweed came to a gaping cave and stopped. Into the cave Bogweed drove sheep and dogs. Into the cave Bogweed carried the sack that held Joe. Then he came out and blocked the mouth of the cave with a huge boulder that ten men couldn't move, and he laughed hugely.

'See now, you silly little man, see what you get for walking along Mastiles Lane when Bogweed forbids it,' roared the giant. 'I'm going to collect firewood now, and I'll roast you and your sheep tonight, and then see what a feast I'll have! Ho! Ho! Such a feast!' Bogweed's bestial laughter

boomed into the caves and shook the bats as they slept on the walls. Then he strode quickly away to the north.

As soon as Bogweed's head had dropped below the horizon, Willie came out of his hiding place, and walked fearfully up to the blocked cave.

'Father, father, can you hear me? It's Willie, your boy Willie.'

So faintly that Willie had to hold his breath to hear, came the answer, 'Willie, dear, can it be you? Yes, I hear you. Are you a prisoner, too?'

'No, father, I'm free. Now listen, I must hurry before Bogweed comes back. Do not fear being eaten by that giant! I will rescue you. I have a plan. Fear not. Did you hear me?'

'Yes, yes, I heard. But how. . . how can a little fellow like you rescue us? How. . .'

'I cannot stop to explain. I must go,' called Willie, fearing to hear Bogweed returning. 'Goodbye for now, fear not!' And Willie fled away, to a good hiding place and a safe distance, though he could watch the cave and the path that he expected Bogweed to use.

Willie knew the moors better than anyone, except Giant Bogweed. All his boyhood years he had explored them endlessly. Perhaps, he hoped, perhaps he knew them even better than Bogweed for there were places where a giant could never go, but where little Willie, light-footed and small as he was, could go safely. There were caves that Willie knew, caves you could drop a cathedral into, so vast they were. There were bogs that Willie knew, dangerously deep bogs, so lightly crusted that anyone but a small boy would founder in them. Yes, Willie knew the moors, and Willie had a good plan. Now he must wait, watching ceaselessly as he had watched for wild creatures many a time; he must wait for Bogweed's return.

After many patient hours, Willie was rewarded. Bogweed came lumbering across the sky-line carrying a great load of wood – trees, broken fences and dry bracken. Gleefully, the giant built a bonfire near the cave, licking his chops and singing a feasting song. Willie crouched, heart thumping, waiting until Bogweed took out his tinder-box to light the fire. Then he jumped out of hiding and shouted as loudly as he could, 'Silly old Bogweed! Stupid, ugly, smelly old Bogweed! Fungus face! Goggle-eyes! Slobberjaws! Turnip nose! Coward, let's see you fight me!'

Slowly, Bogweed stood up. Bemused, he looked about him, to see where the din was coming from. Then he saw Willie.

'What?' he roared. 'Do you dare to insult great Bogweed? Why, I'll roast you alive. I'll. . . I'll. . .'

Willie chanted on, 'Silly Bogweed, you couldn't suck a toffee, your teeth are all falling out. Stinking, nasty old Bogweed, catch me if you can!' And Willie was away across the heather, as fast as he could go, leaping across pools and tussocks, running desperately.

'Why, I'll catch you without even running,' shouted Bogweed, and he came striding after Willie. Having said this, Bogweed was too proud to run, but he was surprised to find that Willie was drawing away from him. Away across the moor went the two of them, until Bogweed decided he'd better run anyway to get the chase over, for he was feeling hungry and wanted to get on with his feast. So he broke into a lumbering run and Willie thought he was done for; then, just in time, Willie found the bog he had been looking for. With light steps he pranced out across the quaking surface. Bogweed was in too great a hurry to stop and look where he was going and his massive feet plunged straight into the bog. The surface sucked down under him, like an egg-shell. Down went Bogweed, down

into the deepest bog in all Yorkshire. He was up to his knees and fighting the sticky mud. Down he went, up to his waist now, with his great arms thrashing about. Willie leapt safely ahead on the trembling crust, on to firm ground. He stood to watch the giant's terrible struggle. As Bogweed's head went down into the mud, Willie thought he must be finished, and began to feel sorry for him; but Bogweed's head came up again, with a roar. Deep as the bog was, Bogweed's great feet had found its bottom. Slowly, striving through depths of black mud that would have drowned a hundred men and left no sign, slowly Bogweed came at Willie, through the bog. Now he was more dreadful than ever, glaring out from a thick mask of mud, and Willie leaped away again across the moor, running for his life.

'Drown me, would you? You little wasp, you led me into that on purpose! I'll tear you to pieces, I will,' bellowed Bogweed, and on he came.

Now Willie knew of only one chance left to him. Swiftly, he ran to a hillside he knew well. There were no bogs there; he knew he couldn't catch Giant Bogweed with that trick again. No, it was a dry hillside with many limestone rocks sticking out of the thin grass. Willie knew that limestone meant caves, a countryside as hollow as a sponge with caves and tunnels and winding underground rivers. The ground underfoot could be drum-hollow and sudden gaping holes opened amongst the tussocks of grass. Willie knew a rapid stream called Gordale Beck. It dropped down into a hole in the ground and splashed into a vast cave. He was near it now. He had a notion about that cave and he carefully led the giant toward it. The weight of the mud that clung to his clothes slowed Bogweed down giving Willie more time. Could he reach Gordale Beck in time? Willie, himself, was becoming tired and short of breath. On he ran, towards his final hope, with the muddy giant cursing and slithering after him and coming rapidly nearer. Suddenly, Gordale Beck was at Willie's feet and he jumped across it, then ran beyond the spot where it dropped into the ground. Bogweed was above him now, on a rock that jutted out from the hillside.

'Come on, jump down and you'll catch me,' taunted Willie. 'Come on, you great fool! Are you too much of a coward to jump?'

This was too much for Bogweed. He let out a screech of rage and jumped from the rock. Willie skipped aside in an unexpected direction, back the way he had come. Surely he would be caught that way? Bogweed thumped down on to the rock and reached out his hand to grab Willie.

But what was this? The ground was crumpling
like paper under Bogweed's feet. A deep
underground roar shook the earth, like an
earthquake. The ground was moving, the rock
dissolving like the surface of a lake! Willie leaped
away and clung to a tree that grew on the side of
the higher rock. Desperately, Bogweed scrambled
for a firm footing. Too late! The ground opened

under his feet and he dropped swiftly into a gaping blackness. A distant cry, and a shattering crash of falling rocks, and Giant Bogweed was gone and dead forever!

The moving earth settled into its new bed. Willie could hear a lark singing, as high above as the giant was deep below. All was quiet. Limestone dust hung in the air. Willie clung to his tree, looked down and saw that his legs were dangling into a great emptiness. He climbed up the tree on to firm ground. He sat for a while, resting and gazing on the changed landscape. For the whole hillside was different. Where there had been a smooth hill, with fields of sheep, there was now a deep gash cut into the earth, a deep scar like a gigantic slash of a sword. The roof of the enormous underground cave, the cave that Gordale Beck had tumbled into for millions of years, the roof – that Giant Bogweed had jumped down upon – the whole roof had fallen in, opening the cave to the light of day. The cave's floor was littered with the shattered rocks that had fallen and the water trickled down amongst them. There was no sign of Bogweed; he was buried deep, deep under the rocks.

When Willie found himself at last, quite unhurt, though shaken and amazed, he went off to the village as fast as he could go. He told the whole story to a gasping crowd, then collapsed with weariness. While his mother put him to bed, a gang of thirty strong men set out with ropes and levers to the cave that Willie had described. Joe, his sheep and his dogs were soon released from their prison, and came blinking into the open air.

'Eh, but I'm glad to be out of that,' said Joe. 'What time is it? Is there time to get to Grassington Fair?'

'Nay, Joe, can you think of nothing but yon fair?' said Bob Varley. 'It's far too late for that, anyway. You'd best get home and see to that brave lad of yours, and your Elsie that's worried to death with the two of you having been gone so long.'

'Well, maybe you're right,' said Joe. 'But I mean to go next week, mind you. Come on, then, let's get home. I'm dying for a drink and a bite to eat.' So off they all went, driving the sheep before them. As they went along, Bob told Joe all that had happened while he had been bottled up in the cave. They all came into the village singing joyously, and it was the cheeriest sound that had been heard in Malham for a hundred years. With the evil giant dead, the people of Malham were the happiest in all Yorkshire.

From that day on, the spot where Giant Bogweed fell was called Gordale Scar. You can go there today and see it just as it was then – it hasn't changed a bit. The rocks are still jumbled about the way Bogweed brought them crashing down. You would be well advised not to go jumping about too much: there may be deeper caves, with fragile roofs, just under your feet.

Six

The story of Giant Dumpling and how he became a hero

There once was a place called Honeytown. It was in a wide valley, full of sunshine and the scent of flowers and the drowsy hum of bees. All round the town, as far as you could see, the land was covered with orchards and gardens and rich farms. Hundreds of beehives stood under the fruit trees and Honeytown was famous for its honey-market. You could not find a more pleasant spot in all the world. Visitors thought it strange to find a giant living in such a place, but there had been a giant in Honeytown as long as anyone could remember. Old Gaskin was a hundred years old, and he could remember the giant being there when he was a boy at school, and his grandfather knew the giant when he was a boy. No one could miss seeing the giant's home; it was an enormous cavern on the edge of the town with a wide road leading to it. Everyone called him Giant Dumpling, because he was so fat and so round, and everyone was fond of him because he was a good and kind giant. He would do anything to help the people of Honeytown. He would stamp down the earth for new roads, move trees when they needed replanting, dig foundations for new houses; nothing was too much trouble. In return, the people gave him barrels of honey, which he loved more than anything else, and which made him so fat. Giant Dumpling even said that if the people of Honeytown ever had enemies, he would fight them and drive them away.

Honeytown lived in peace for many, many years, for, as Old Gaskin often said, 'Who would dare to attack a town with a giant living in it? Nobody in his senses would do such a thing. Giant Dumpling would soon scare them away.'

'What about those people the other side of Moss River?' his young grandson, Peter, would ask.

'The Mosslanders?' Old Gaskin would growl. 'They'd never dare trouble us. Our honey-sellers visit Mossland, and they spread stories about how fierce Giant Dumpling is, to frighten the Mosslanders, strange folks that they are.'

'But Giant Dumpling isn't fierce,' Peter would protest, 'he's good and gentle. He plays with the children and gets fat eating honey. I believe he's too fat to run, let alone fight.'

'Hush, boy! Hush, boy!' Old Gaskin would say

then, and send Peter out to gather peaches.

The years went by; years of peace and good living for Honeytown; years of hardship and thin living for the Mosslanders. Giant Dumpling grew fatter and rounder with each year that passed and Peter Gaskin worried still about their giant's real usefulness for keeping enemies away if it should ever come to a real battle. Peter grew to be a man, to have his own fruit-farm and keep his own bees. One day in autumn, he was busy about the farm when a Mosslander came to buy honey. He was a darkbrowed fellow, big and strong, though haggard and hungry looking, called Guntrop Gilliform. He stood in the farmyard with his two-horse wagon, frowning at Peter Gaskin. The barrels of honey were loaded on to the wagon and tied down securely. Now Peter waited for Guntrop to pay him, but Guntrop did not get out his purse, he just stood glaring at Peter as though he hated him.

'We've had a terrible harvest in Mossland, terrible,' said Guntrop, looking as though he thought it was Peter's fault. 'We're going to starve this winter, in Mossland.'

'I'm truly sorry to hear it,' said Peter. 'There have been rumours. . .'

'And here are you Honeytowners, living like princes,' growled Guntrop, looking about him. 'Look at it all, the richest land I ever saw! So much food that you can even keep that great fool of a giant in honey!'

'How dare you talk of our giant like that,' said Peter angrily. 'He's a good giant; the best there is. He's protected us from our enemies for hundreds of years, he's. . .'

'Enemies!' sneered Guntrop. 'Protected you from your enemies? He's too fat! He couldn't knock the skin off a rice pudding. A hundred years ago, when he was younger and thinner – maybe he could fight then – fifty years ago, even, but not now, oh no, not now.'

'All this is nonsense. He happens to be our giant, and no concern of yours,' retorted Peter. 'We'll feed him as we want and not ask you.'

'No concern of ours, is he,' snarled Guntrop. 'We'll see about that, we will.'

'What do you mean by that?' demanded Peter.

'Never you mind,' said Guntrop darkly.

'Well, pay me for the honey, please, and go on your way,' said Peter. 'I have work to do. I cannot afford to spend the day in idle gossip, even if you can.'

'Gossip? Pay?' shouted Guntrop. 'You'll see, you will. You've got a big shock coming to you. As for payment for the honey, you can take this!' He snatched up his big horse-whip and lashed Peter hard about the legs. Peter cried out with pain, and fell to the ground. Guntrop leaped upon his wagon, shouted wildly at the horses and whipped them into a mad gallop. The wagon shot out of the farmyard, gathering speed, and went swaying dangerously down the road, tilting round the corner with a desperate scrabbling of hooves, and was gone.

Slowly, Peter picked himself up out of the dust and hobbled painfully into the house.

As soon as Peter felt well enough, he saddled his best horse and rode into town with all speed. He went straight to the Mayor and told him all that had happened. The Mayor looked grave at Peter's news. He said, 'Your tale is bad enough, Peter Gaskin, it is only one of many. From every part of our land stories have been brought to me of Mosslanders attacking and robbing our innocent people.'

'Worst of all,' cried Peter, 'they have no fear of Giant Dumpling any more.'

'We'll see about that,' said the Mayor, 'but you know what this means, don't you? It means war. War with the Mosslanders, for they will come and take our land from us if we do nothing. I'm making a proclamation this very hour. Every able-bodied man is to have his sword and bow to hand and be ready to march at eight o'clock tomorrow morning.'

'So soon?' said Peter.

'It cannot be soon enough. We must defend

ourselves before the Mosslanders have a chance to cross Moss Bridge. Once they cross the river we're lost. We wouldn't stand a chance.'

'But Giant Dumpling would defend us,' said Peter.

'I fear that Guntrop was only too near the truth,' sighed the Mayor. 'Poor old Dumpling *is* very fat and he's not a fierce giant, alas; never was, and never will be. You cannot keep that kind of thing a secret for ever and the Mosslanders have found it out at last. Still, you never can be sure, he may be of some use, so we'll take him along with us. If he isn't fierce he is strong; after all he is a giant. Come, let's go and see him.'

The Mayor called his Council and his General, and they all trooped off to see Giant Dumpling, followed by a growing crowd of Honeytowners.

Giant Dumpling was having a nap when the crowd arrived at his cave and it took a great deal of knocking and shouting to waken him. He came at last to his door, sleepily rubbing his eyes.

'What's all the noise?' he rumbled. 'Can't you let a fellow have his sleep in peace? Ooh, what a lot of people! Hello Mr Mayor. Hello General Galt, what are you doing in your uniform? And all you fellows with swords, what are you up to? You want to be careful – nasty things swords, I can't abide them – you'll be hurting somebody with those things if you're not careful. Oooh, and bows too, worse and worse. Now you really shouldn't play at soldiers. . .'

'Giant Dumpling, we're not *playing*...' shouted General Galt.

'. . . it really is much too dangerous,' pursued Giant Dumpling. 'Eat honey and grow good fruit, that's the best way to live. Now put these nasty things away and let me have my sleep and come back when you can be sensible.'

'Giant Dumpling,' shouted General Galt, louder still, 'we're not playing at soldiers. All this is serious. The Mosslanders are about to attack. We must stop them crossing the river. Moss Bridge is our only hope of defence.'

'Oh, well, that's different,' said Giant Dumpling. 'Off you go and have your battle and wake me up when it's all over.'

'Oh no, we want you to help us,' protested the Mayor. 'We haven't kept you in honey all these years for you to go off to bed at the first sign of a battle. What's the use of having a real giant if you can't fight for us!'

'Oh dear. I'm not really a warlike giant,' wailed Dumpling.

'Surely you can *look* fierce, even if you don't do any fighting?' asked Peter.

'I don't think I can even do that,' moaned Dumpling.

'There's not another drop of honey for you if you don't come to Moss Bridge with us in the morning,' said the Mayor sternly.

'Then I'll have to come, I suppose,' wailed Dumpling, 'though I'd much rather stay at home and read a good book, I really would. Oh, but I'll come, if you insist, though what use I'll be I cannot guess. I've never held a sword in my life and I wouldn't know how to fire an arrow.'

'You can stamp and make the ground shake and roar like thunder and put such fear into the Mosslanders that they'll not dare to cross that bridge,' General Galt suggested.

'I'll do my best, but I don't promise anything, mind you,' said Dumpling. And with that they let him go back to his bed, tut-tutting and shaking his head.

The scene at Moss Bridge early the next day was one that every Honeytowner would remember to the end of his days. Moss River was the boundary between the Honeytowners' lands and the bare acres of Mossland, and a swift and wide river it was. Moss Bridge was the only way of crossing the river. It was a wooden bridge that arched gracefully over the tumbling waters and it was wide enough for two laden wagons to pass each other, with room to spare. The Honeytown army reached the bridge soon after nine o'clock having made good speed along their excellent roads. They marched smartly along, with their helmets glittering in the sun. The footsoldiers came first, then the cavalry, then the horsedrawn cannons, then the supply train of donkeys and mules and the field-kitchens. Last of all, behind the rearmost donkey-boy, came Giant Dumpling, lagging behind and trying to look as though he had nothing at all to do with the army. True, he did wear a sword, but it was so rusty that anyone could see that it would never come out of its scabbard. Twice Giant Dumpling had tried to turn back, saying he'd forgotten something important, but each time General Galt had called him back into line. He trudged along now, looking out nervously for any sign of Mosslanders. Though he was far away at the back of the army, Giant Dumpling was so tall that he would see the enemy long before anyone else.

'Any sign of the Mosslanders?' shouted General Galt.

'Not a single one, thank goodness,' said Giant Dumpling.

The army marched over the bridge. The cannons took up positions by the river, on the Honeytown side, and the men began to dig them in, ready to give covering fire over the heads of their own men. The cavalry trotted over the bridge in good order. The mules and donkeys ambled over the bridge, not hurrying for anyone. Last of all, and full of trembling fear, fat and shaking, Giant Dumpling crossed over the bridge.

The cooks lit their fires, and the smoke curled high into the still air, and there was a good smell of frying bacon. General Galt was just about to eat a boiled egg, when there was a great BOOOOOOM from a belt of trees some way off, and a dozen cannon-balls came swishing through the air towards the Honeyland camp. They all fell harmlessly into the river, raising great spouts of water. Giant Dumpling began hopping about near the water.

'Oh my stars!' he exclaimed. 'Oh, bless me! Oh dear, dear, dear, we'll all be killed, that's for sure. Those dreadful Mosslanders, they're *shooting* at us.'

'Well, it *is* a war!' exploded General Galt. 'Do you expect them to throw flowers? For goodness' sake, Giant Dumpling, do try to look brave and fierce even if you cannot feel it.'

At that moment the Honeyland cannons opened fire. Being so near, they made an earth-shaking BANG. This gave Giant Dumpling such a fright that he fainted on the spot. His great body dropped like a falling tower, with a deafening SPLASH, into the river. He was so big, and so fat, that he filled the river from bank to bank; and the tremendous splash he made, sent a wave as high as a house racing down the river. The great wave sped towards Moss Bridge. The wave hit the bridge, and there was a tearing and rending and splintering of wood, and the bridge disappeared under a seething mass of water. The great wave smashed onward. The water subsided. There was no bridge.

'The bridge's down!' shouted General Galt. 'We're trapped! We cannot get back to Honeytown!'

'Oh yes we can,' said Peter Gaskin. 'Look, sir, Giant Dumpling's dammed the river, he's so fat. We can retreat across the river bed – it's almost dry – or we can use Giant Dumpling himself as a bridge.'

'BOOOOM. BOOOOM. BOOOOM.' The Mossland cannons were firing steadily now, and the balls fell uncomfortably close.

'Quick, sir, before Giant Dumpling gets up!' shouted Peter.

'Sound the retreat,' ordered General Galt, and all along the line the trumpets shrilly answered him, 'Retreat! Retreat!' in their own tongue.

The cavalry galloped across the dry river-bed. The foot-soldiers climbed with all speed across Giant Dumpling's gently breathing body. The mules and donkeys, struggling with heavy loads, were last across, scrambling over the stones of the

dry river. Then the Mossland army appeared, galloping at full speed towards the river, waving their swords and shouting in triumph.

'We've downed their giant! Their giant's dead! Charge! Kill the Honeytowners! Take all their land! Charge! Charge!'

Seeing that the river was now dry they galloped still faster, straight towards the dismayed Honeytowners, who stood ready to take the full force of their assault. The Mosslanders plunged into the river-bed. They were so near now that the Honeytowners could see the evil light of battle in their faces, the eagerness to kill, and a chill fear struck at the Honeytowners' hearts. Giant Dumpling chose this very moment to get up. With many a groan, he lumbered to his feet, climbing out of the deep river bed. The great river, which had been piling up behind him, was released, and it swept down upon the Mosslanders now with all its pent-up force. They began to turn back. Too late! The deep water was upon them. They were engulfed and swept away before they had time to draw breath to shout a warning. The swift river ran on, tossing a few wooden spears to its surface. The Mossland army was gone, without so much as a cry. The Honeytowners stood in stunned silence on the river bank.

'Poor fellows. Poor fellows,' said General Galt.

'They would have killed us, sir,' said Peter.

'I know it, I know it, my boy, but it's a sad, sad business,' General Galt answered.

Meanwhile Giant Dumpling was finding himself, feeling for the dreadful wound he was sure he had suffered, wailing and moaning on the river side.

'My poor head. My poor head. They've shot me, sure enough, and look at my poor clothes, all wet and muddy. If I'm not shot I'll catch my death of cold, lying in that nasty cold river all this while. Oh, deary me.'

'You're not wounded, Giant Dumpling,' said the Mayor.

'Not wounded?' said Giant Dumpling, staring in disbelief.

'No, you. . . well you sort of fainted when our guns went off,' said the Mayor.

'Fainted? I *fainted*? Dear, oh dear. So now I'm in disgrace for being a coward,' moaned Giant Dumpling.

'No, no, no, not at all,' said the Mayor. 'You're the hero of the day.'

'The hero?'

'Yes, you've won the battle, and saved us all from a horrible death.'

'Won? Saved?' murmured Giant Dumpling, too bemused to put two words together, but beginning to smile.

'Yes, dear fellow,' said the Mayor. 'You tell him, General, you're better at battles than I am.'

So General Galt told Giant Dumpling the whole story and made him a Field-Marshal on the spot. They dried his clothes over a big fire and they all marched home joyfully, this time with Giant Dumpling leading, looking as pleased as could be. When they reached Honeytown the whole town sang and feasted far into the night and the people cheered Giant Dumpling until his head spun.

That was the happiest day of Giant Dumpling's long life. The people gave him all the honey he wanted and he certainly grew no thinner. As Peter said, 'If he hadn't been so fat, he couldn't have won the battle.'

Moss Bridge was never rebuilt, and the river was so feared that no one would venture on it in a boat, so the Honeytowners were safe from the Mosslanders, thanks to their unwarlike giant. They grew their fruit and tended their bees and never thought of war again.

Giant Dumpling lived to a ripe and contented old age: there was no happier giant in all the world. Years and years afterwards, he would tell the story of the great battle when he became a famous hero, just as it is written here.

Seven

Giant Mambrino and the Pendle witches

There was once a giant called Mambrino who lived near Pendle Hill in Lancashire. Now Pendle Hill was famous for the witches who lived on and around it, but Mambrino was a peaceful fellow. He didn't trouble the witches and they didn't trouble him. They took care to keep out of each other's way. This arrangement worked very well, until the day Mambrino invented a new game. It happened when Grundy came over from Yorkshire to spend a holiday with Mambrino. Grundy was a giant too, and had been Mambrino's best friend since they had been boys together at school. Whenever they were together they remembered the jokes and pranks of their schooldays and they became full of glee and mischief.

One sunny morning, Mambrino and Grundy were walking on the slopes of Pendle Hill when they saw some old millstones lying about on the grass; hefty discs of stone, five or six feet across,

they were.

'Bet you can't roll one of those fellows over the hill,' said Mambrino.

'Easy,' said Grundy. 'Easy as marbles.'

'Go on then, let's see you,' said Mambrino.

'Easy,' said Grundy, and he picked one of the stones up and weighed it in his hand. 'Tell you what, let's have a competition. First to roll three right over the top wins. Loser has to buy ten barrels of beer for the winner.'

'You're on,' cried Mambrino.

Each giant balanced a millstone carefully in his hand and measured the height of the hill with his eye. Pendle is a good shape for bowling millstones: nicely rounded, with no cliffs or sharp points, though it is high enough.

'One, two, three–go!' shouted the giants together.

Two great millstones rolled up the hill, smashing their way through bushes and bracken. The earth shook with their thunderous rolling. Sheep leapt for their lives out of their path. A terrified shepherd narrowly missed being smashed to splinters. But the silly giants gave no thought to the danger; they leaped about, shouting with excitement, urging their millstones on.

'Go on! Over you go!' bellowed Grundy.

'Come on, my beauty, don't stop!' thundered Mambrino.

The stones went more and more slowly and stopped a good way short of the top. Eagerly, the giants grabbed more stones. They swung them mightily and again the terrible stones crashed up the hillside. This time Grundy was jubilant.

'Mine's gone over! Mine's gone over!' he yelled. Mambrino's had fallen short.

'Just wait. I'll show you,' growled Mambrino, and he flung the next stone with all his might. It crashed over the hill and out of view. They could hear it smashing and splintering down the other side.

'You've seen nothing yet,' shouted Grundy. He took a millstone in each hand and bowled them both furiously at the hillside. One stuck in a bog but the other went over. Faster and faster the giants bowled the stones, getting more and more excited.

All this time, terror was spreading amongst the people who lived on the other side of the hill. They had to leap and run for their lives as the stones came thundering down the hillside. Nothing could stop them. They smashed down walls, cottages and farms; they left a trail of dead cows and sheep behind them. The people ran, leaving their farms and villages to be destroyed.

When Grundy and Mambrino had used all the stones, they came racing round the hill to pick them up and begin again. When they saw the litter of dead creatures, broken walls and smashed houses, they stopped short.

'Have we done that?' said Grundy.

'We can't have – it was only a game,' said Mambrino. 'Oh, dear, I think we have, though,' wailed Grundy, looking stricken.

'We'd better get away from here,' said Mambrino, beginning to quail. 'There are numerous witches living about here and if we've smashed any of their cottages. . .'

'Too late! Too late!' A harsh voice grated in their ears. Too late indeed! The whole coven of witches was about them crackling with anger, like a darkly sinister nest of wasps. Their leader, Old Mother Dubkin, screeched at the two giants.

'You great stupid buffoons, do you know what you've done?'

'It was only a game,' wailed Mambrino.

'A game? A game?' rasped Old Mother Dubkin. 'Do you call it a game to knock the end of my house off with your great stones and scatter my spells and potions to the four winds? All gone; the work of twenty years whisked away in a twinkling!'

'Yes, and my house too! And mine! And mine!' Voice after voice was raised in anger against them.

'And what about the poor people in these parts?' demanded Old Mother Dubkin. 'Sheep and cattle dead by the score. They'll say *we've* done it with our spells. Yes, they'll blame us, sure enough, we're blamed for all evil that befalls. Then they'll chase us out of the country, or burn us at the stake, and much you'll care, you enormous fools!'

'We didn't mean any harm,' protested Giant Grundy. 'Harm?' snapped Old Mother Dubkin. 'Harm, you say? Well we do mean harm; harm to

you. We're going to punish you in a way that you'll never forget. Come, sisters, weave your spells! Bind these dangerous giants in delicious torment!'

Then a muttering arose amongst the black brood of witches as they cast their evil spells against the giants. And the giants stood there, stricken with terror, for they found that they could not move a single muscle, no matter how much they strained against the magic. A whole coven of witches was too much, even for such mighty giants as they were. Stuck where they stood, unable to run away or stay and fight, pure fear overcame the giants, and bitter tears gushed from their eyes. Then the torments began. Prickings, bitings, stingings, burnings and scratchings seared through the whole of their bodies. Wicked cramps cracked their bones. Their teeth sang with pain. Their eyeballs burnt like hot coals. Then Old Mother Dubkin raised both hands and called in a cold voice – 'Stay your magic, sisters. Release these giants from torment. I would have words with them. They have learnt a good lesson now.'

All the pains melted away and the giants could move again. Poor Mambrino. Poor Grundy! They groaned fit to burst the heavens. They rubbed their afflicted arms and legs. They dried their eyes and mopped their brows.

'That was a foul punishment,' moaned Grundy.

'No worse than the hurt you did to us and to the good people hereabouts,' snapped Old Mother Dubkin. 'Now, see you here, Grundy and Mambrino. You will make good all the damage you have done. You will mend all the walls and fences and rebuild every farm, house and cottage. You will give the good people gold out of your store so that they can buy new sheep and cattle. If you do not do as I say, we will visit you with torments far worse than the ones you have just endured.'

'Oh, anything but that!' wailed Grundy.

'We'll do all you say,' whimpered Mambrino. 'We'll put all to rights. You'll see.'

'We'll set about it at once,' said Grundy in a servile voice.

'Wait a moment. There is one more thing,' grinned Old Mother Dubkin. 'You will both wear a millstone, hung on a rope around your neck, for a year from this day, to show true penitence.'

'Would you shame us, too,' moaned Grundy.

'Yours is the shame; yours to show it,' answered Old Mother Dubkin. 'And so farewell. Remember – our eyes will be on you!'

With a rustle like the leathery wings of bats, the whole coven of witches rose into the sky, and flew off to the East.

Grundy and Mambrino tied millstones round their necks, and their weight dragged at them and wearied them, as they bent to the task of mending all the damage they had done. Perhaps their heads were bowed even more by shame than by the millstones but the people soon took pity on them. As soon as they knew all danger had past, they came back to their villages and farms and helped the giants in the work of repair. They gave the giants buckets of strong tea, or beer, to refresh and cheer them. They encouraged them with kind words.

It took the giants twenty days of hard work to complete their task. Then they brought gold for the new sheep and cattle. Then they trod off home sadly. Never has the world seen a sadder pair of giants!

Grundy refused to go home to Yorkshire with a millstone round his neck, so he stayed the whole year with Mambrino.

'We might as well be miserable together,' he said.

They cheered up a lot when the year was up and they could take the millstones off. They carried them to the top of Pendle and buried them deep under the ground, where no one would ever find them.

The other millstones are still scattered about

the fields at the foot of Pendle Hill. Some are buried and farmers curse when their ploughs catch on them. Some lie on the surface and curious people stop a moment to wonder how they got there.

Eight

The giant who stole the world

Once there was a giant.

He was a big giant.

He was a *very* big giant.

One day he found a ball spinning in the sky. He plucked it from the sky and put it in his pocket. He was so big that he didn't know what it was. It was, indeed, the world!

It was dark in the giant's pocket and the people on the world thought that night had come. The giant's pocket had holes in it, and they looked like stars. It had one big hole and that looked like the moon. The people who were in bed just went on sleeping. The people who were up and about, in the daytime half of the world, were very upset.

'It *isn't* bedtime! We've only just got up!' wailed the children, as their mothers began putting them to bed.

'But look, the sky is dark, and the stars are shining, whatever the clock says,' said the mothers; and it was true. So the children went to

bed. And all the birds and flowers went to sleep too. In the factories, the nightworkers went to work and got all mixed up with the dayworkers. All the daytime buses and trains stopped running, so that almost everyone had to walk home. The cows refused to be milked but just slept in their stalls. The teachers in the schools had no children to teach and sat doing sums all by themselves. The television people began sending out the evening programmes.

It was *chaos*.

People asked each other, 'How can night come in the middle of the day?' None knew the answer. Until the Head of Television had an idea.

'We must ask an astronomer,' he said; 'sun and stars, day and night; it's his job to know all about them. Find the Astronomer Royal! Interview him! Ask him all your questions! Hurry!'

So a television unit, with cameras and microphones, lights and a big flask of coffee, hurried out across the dark countryside to the Royal Observatory. There, the Astronomer Royal was gazing through his biggest telescope with a puzzled expression on his face. When all the television men burst in on him, upsetting his cup of tea and a pile of notes, he became flustered and cross and said he wouldn't go on television to answer their silly questions; but they pointed their cameras at him anyway, so he just had to. Soon, all the people saw his face on their television screens. They anxiously awaited his answer to the mystery.

The television man spoke first, 'Everyone's worried and upset about night coming in the middle of the day. The country's in chaos. Can you tell us, Sir William, what can have caused this to happen?'

'Bless me, you don't give a man time to think,' said Sir William. 'I've been at my telescope all night, I mean all day; oh dear, what a muddle! Well, the only thing that *can* make the sun go dark in the daytime is a total eclipse of the sun. The next one is due to happen at half past one on Thursday afternoon, just ten years from now. So it cannot be an eclipse!'

'What *can* it be, Sir William?' said the television man.

'How do I know,' exclaimed the Astronomer Royal crossly. 'I don't know the answer to everything. I do know there's something funny about the stars. They're frayed at the edges, like cloth!'

'Frayed! But that's impossible!' said the television man.

'See for yourselves,' said the Astronomer Royal.

The television man poked his camera into the big telescope, so that everyone could see through it. There was a star, and sure enough, it was frayed at the edges!

'Now look at this other one,' said the Astronomer Royal, as he moved the telescope across the sky. 'Bless me, but it looks as if it's been darned!'

'Darned!' shouted the television man. 'But that's preposterous! It's ridiculous! Who ever heard of a star *darned* like an old sock! It's the funniest thing I ever heard.'

And he began to laugh, and laugh, and he couldn't stop. The Astronomer Royal began to laugh. All the people watching began to laugh. Clearly enough they could all see a darned star, with giant stitches across one side. Soon, half the people in the world were laughing, and the children laughed themselves out of bed when they heard of it. As soon as he could speak, the Astronomer Royal spluttered, 'That's bad enough, but what about the smell of cheese!'

'*Cheese?*' everyone gasped.

'Yes, cheese,' he said; 'there's a strong smell of cheese everywhere. Haven't you noticed?'

And he was right. People began telephoning the observatory from all over the world to say that they could smell cheese everywhere. It was on the mountains and in the valleys; it was on the seas and by the rivers; it was all over the plains and downs; it was at the North Pole and the South Pole, the Tropics and the Equator; it could be smelt from Ormskirk to Mexico City: it was everywhere! All the world smelt of cheese, and no one knew why.

All this time the giant was walking along with the world in his pocket. The holes in his pocket were frayed and darned. He had also put a large piece of cheese in the same pocket. When he got home, the giant said to his boy, 'Come and see what I have in my pocket. You'll never guess what it is!'

His boy came and looked curiously. The giant took the world out of his pocket, and threw it, spinning, into the sky. It went away up into the sky and didn't come down.

'That's a pretty ball,' said the giant's boy.

At that moment, day came back to the world.

The children got out of bed and went to school.

The cows awoke and let themselves be milked.

The birds and the flowers woke up.

The night-workers went home.

The buses and trains began running again.

The Astronomer Royal pushed all the television men out of his observatory and locked the door.

People sniffed and sniffed, but the cheesy smell was gone.

The world was once more as it should be.

But no one could even begin to guess why night had come in the middle of day, why frayed and darned stars had been seen in the sky, or why all the world had smelt of cheese.

Nine

Giant Gorongoro's handkerchief

There was a giant who lived, a long time ago, in a hot desert in North Africa. His name was Gorongoro. He had no clothes, because he lived at a time before the giants knew how to make looms big enough to weave giant cloth. He didn't need clothes because it was so hot in the desert, and in the cold desert nights he had a warm cave to sleep in. But one thing he did need was a handkerchief; poor old Gorongoro had a sore and sniffy nose and no soft and smooth handkerchief to soothe it. It was dusty in the desert; the winds swirled the dust about and made Gorongoro sneeze; his poor nose became red and tender and he had no way of helping it. In despair he went to the little town at the foot of the mountains and asked the people if they had any very big pieces of cloth they could sell him. The head man of the town was called Abdul Aziz and he came out upon the flat roof of his house to speak with Gorongoro. The giant knelt down and bent his ear down to Abdul, who called up to him,

'Oh Gorongoro! What is it that ails you? Why do you want a big piece of cloth? You know we cannot weave cloth big enough to make clothes for a person of your magnificent size.'

'I know that,' boomed Gorongoro. 'It isn't clothes I want. I only want a handkerchief. It's my poor nose, you see; my poor sore nose!' And he told Abdul Aziz all about his nose.

'Yes, I see how sore it is,' said Abdul, peering up at that great nose, itself the size of a camel, all red and inflamed. 'It's the biggest soreness I ever saw. What a torment it must be! I feel for you, Gorongoro, but I fear there's little we can do to help. Let me see, now, would a table-cloth be big enough?' He called the ladies of the house, and they brought out their biggest tablecloth, and held it out for Gorongoro to take. He picked it up delicately between finger and thumb and applied it to his nose. One sniff and the table-cloth disappeared into Gorongoro's left nostril and was never seen again.

'You see?' moaned Gorongoro.

'Yes, I see,' said Abdul; 'we've lost our best tablecloth.'

'Our best table-cloth. Our best table-cloth,' twittered the ladies. 'Swallowed by that great fellow.'

'I'm sorry,' said Gorongoro. 'I'll pay you for it.' And he placed an enormous coin on the ground. Then he looked up at the blue dome of the sky. 'I've been thinking,' he said. 'The sky is big enough, and smooth enough to make me a handkerchief, if I could cut out a piece of it with my sword. It's a pretty colour, too.'

'You musn't cut a hole in the sky,' said Abdul. 'You'll let all the evil spirits in from outside. You'll let all the blackness and coldness of the universe pour in upon us by day as well as by night.'

'You cannot stop me,' said Gorongoro.

'No, but I beg you not to do it,' said Abdul. 'The evil spirits will fall upon *you*, no less than anyone else.'

'What else can I do,' complained Gorongoro. 'My nose will give me no rest.'

He strode away across the desert, deep in thought, while Abdul shook his head and shooed the ladies indoors.

The next day, Gorongoro was seen climbing the highest mountain in those parts with his sword in his hand. The people in the town trembled for fear of what would happen but Abdul told them to be calm and put their trust in Allah.

Gorongoro climbed up and up, to the very highest peak of the mountain, until he was as near the blue sky as he could be. It was a dry country, so there were no clouds to disturb the sky's blueness. At this height the sky looked prettier than ever. Gorongoro took his enormous sword from its scabbard, reached as high as his long arms would stretch, and began to cut an immense piece out of the sky. As he cut round the second side of the square, a vast piece of blue sky sagged down, showing the deep cold black of outer space in the hole that was left. A chill air fell upon Gorongoro, making him shiver; but he could not stop now, so he went on, cutting and cutting at the sky. At last the square was complete and a great soft blue piece of sky fell down. Gorongoro caught it up and at once put it to his nose. Never, oh never, had he felt anything so smooth, so soft and silky; it soothed and soothed his burning nose in a moment of pure bliss. Then he felt the cold air upon him, the cold that was coming out of the black hole he had made in the sky. He hurried to put his sword away, and tie his new handkerchief safely round his waist, and climb down the mountain away from the coldness. But, alas, he could not get away from the cold. Down below in the sandy desert, it was just as cold as it had been on the mountain; the deep cold from the black hole in the sky struck down and reached him and froze him to his very bones. Gorongoro crept,

shivering, deep into his cave, and lay with his new handkerchief pressed to his nose. Even there the cold reached him. Nowhere could he escape it. Although his nose was a world better, he was even more miserable than before!

The coldness fell, too, upon the people in the little town. All their houses and their clothes were made for the very hot weather that they had all year round in that part of the world. So, when the cold fell from the sky, the people shivered and huddled in their blankets, and were only a little less miserable than the naked Gorongoro himself. When Gorongoro came across the desert the next day, there was no friendly greeting for him in the town. Abdul Aziz strode angrily about the roof of his house, wrapped in blankets and looking blue about the face, waiting for Gorongoro to come within earshot. People pointed at the black hole in the sky, and shook their fists at Gorongoro.

When the giant was near enough, Abdul yelled at him, 'Now, see what you've done, you great ninny! You've got your precious handkerchief, but now we're freezing to death. It's only a matter of time before we all catch a chill and die of pneumonia, or something.'

'Oh, Abdul, please don't be angry with me,' wailed Gorongoro. 'I'm colder than anyone. After all, I have no clothes or blankets; I'm bare to all the dreadful chill. I'll be the first to die.'

'Small comfort will that be to us,' snapped Abdul. 'I did warn you that you could only do harm by cutting the sky to bits. The cold's bad enough, but who can tell what evil spirits are tumbling through that foul hole at this minute!'

'Please forgive me and help me,' begged Gorongoro. 'I never was so miserable in all my life. My nose is better but my whole body is icy. I didn't know this would happen. I thought you were just trying to frighten me.'

'Help you? Help you?' spluttered Abdul. 'Allah, give me strength! What about you helping us?'

'Anything you say,' said Gorongoro. 'I'll do whatever you say.'

'Any fool can see what's to be done,' growled Abdul. 'That hole must be mended, of course, and quickly.'

'But how can that be done?' asked Gorongoro.

'You fathead, you'll have to sew that handkerchief of yours back into the sky.'

'My lovely new handkerchief?'

'Yes, your lovely new handkerchief. Which is worse? To have a sore nose or freeze to death?' demanded Abdul.

'Any fool knows the answer to that,' said Gorongoro.

'Including you,' answered Abdul. 'So we'll have to melt all our swords to make a needle big enough for you to use, and give you miles of our best rope, so that you can sew the sky up again. We'll tell you when we're ready. Don't go far away.'

It took six days for Abdul's people to make the gigantic needle and gather all the rope needed. When all was ready, Abdul sent for Gorongoro, and off he went up the highest mountain again, but this time carrying a needle instead of a sword. His lovely blue handkerchief was tied round his waist and the great coil of rope hung over his shoulder. He was so ill and tired with the days of intense cold that he hardly had the strength to climb the mountain. Up and up, he wearily struggled, until at last he reached the top. After a long rest he raised up the last of his strength, to complete his task. In the town below it had become so cold that it had even begun to snow, and the people prayed to Allah for the giant to succeed in patching the sky in time to save them from being frozen to death.

Hour after hour, Gorongoro worked at his enormous patch. In and out, in and out, went his needle. Slowly the blue handkerchief stretched across to cover the blackness. Slowly the stitches were drawn tight. Slowly the utter cold and blackness were shut out. Far away, in the town, it began to get warm again, and the snow began to melt. Gorongoro's task was at last complete, the sky was well patched and safe again; but poor Gorongoro was quite worn out with the effort, and he slumped down upon the mountain top, and fell into a long deep sleep.

As Gorongoro slept, Abdul was busy in the town. He had seen the finished patch in the sky through his telescope and now he called all his people to the market square to tell them the good news.

'Good people,' he said. 'Gorongoro has patched the sky. We are safe again from the bitter cold. We must show our thanks to Gorongoro, for he is weary almost to death by this great labour. He is sleeping now to rest himself. When he awakes we must give him the handkerchief he so greatly desires.'

A woman spoke from the crowd: 'Lord Abdul, how can this be? No loom of ours can weave cloth of so great a size as to make a giant's handkerchief.'

'True enough,' said Abdul. 'But if each household will give one sheet from their largest bed, and if all the women will sew all the sheets together here in the market place, then we will have a handkerchief fit for a giant.'

A murmur of excitement ran across the crowd and shout after shout rose into the air.

'We'll do it! We'll do it!' People scattered to their homes and soon the bright colours of the bed-sheets began to spread across the square, like sudden tropical blossoms. The town had a thousand households and within the hour a thousand sheets were spread out. A thousand mothers and their two thousand daughters were busily sewing the sheets together. In and out, in and out, flew three thousand needles, glittering in the sun. The biggest handkerchief in the world was finished by sunset. All the men came to admire the wonderful handkerchief and the fine needlework of their womenfolk. The wine-skins were brought out and someone began to play a mandolin. Food was brought and lights. There was drinking and eating and singing and laughter, far into the purple night. The children crept out of their beds, and were allowed to stay. They gathered round the fountain to hear an old man tell stories of the ancient times, of wizards and flying horses, of great heroes and black demons. It was a sudden fiesta, there on the warm expanse of the gigantic handkerchief, a charmed night that none would ever forget.

Gorongoro slept for four days. When he awoke he felt strong again, and very hungry, so he climbed down the mountain, went to his cave and had a good dinner. Then his nose felt sore, so he stretched out his hand for his soft blue handkerchief. It wasn't there! Then he remembered where it was and he felt sad, and old, and grey. He went outside and looked up at the blue sky. Yes, there it was, neatly stitched into place. Poor Gorongoro, his nose felt worse than ever.

'I'd better go and tell Abdul I've put it back,' he said gloomily to himself, 'and give him his needle back.'

Dragging his feet, Gorongoro walked slowly across the desert to the town.

All this time the giant handkerchief lay rolled into a great bundle on the shady side of the market-place, away from the dust and heat. As Gorongoro approached the town, he saw a great gathering of people and hoped they were not angry with him.

Abdul Aziz waited for him on his roof and as soon as he could make Gorongoro hear, he shouted: 'Well done, Gorongoro! You have made an excellent job of mending the sky.'

'You've seen it, then?' said Gorongoro.

'Yes, through my telescope.'

'I'm glad *you're* satisfied,' grumbled Gorongoro. 'As for me, I suppose I don't matter, but my nose is worse than ever.'

'Wait until you see your reward, my dear giant,' smiled Abdul. 'We also have been working hard.' He clapped his hands, and a great crowd of men staggered into view, carrying the rolled-up handkerchief. They laid it at

Gorongoro's feet. 'For you, with our blessing,' said Abdul. Slowly, Gorongoro unrolled the enormous handkerchief. His eyes grew round with astonishment.

'It is pretty,' said Gorongoro. 'What is it?'

'A handkerchief, of your very own, of course. Can you not see what it is?' laughed Abdul.

'A handkerchief? Truly for me?' gasped Gorongoro. 'My very own?' Slowly, he put it to his nose, and soothed it, and closed his eyes with joy. Then he laughed and looked towards Abdul and said, 'You dear, clever people, I cannot guess how you did it. Mind, it's not as smooth as the

sky, but it's good enough for a great rough fellow like me. It will be a blessing when my poor nose sniffles and tickles. Bless you, good people, but what can I do to thank you?'

'Just promise not to cut any more holes in the sky. That will be thanks enough for us,' said Abdul.

'That I do promise you, I will never, ever, do again,' said Gorongoro. He put his new handkerchief to his nose again and his voice came muffled through its folds as he strode away; 'Thank you. Thank you ever so much. It's lovely. Really lovely. Goodbye!'

Gorongoro kept his promise and his patch is still there in the blue sky over the desert, to this very day, but no one notices it because the stitches are so faded as to be almost invisible.